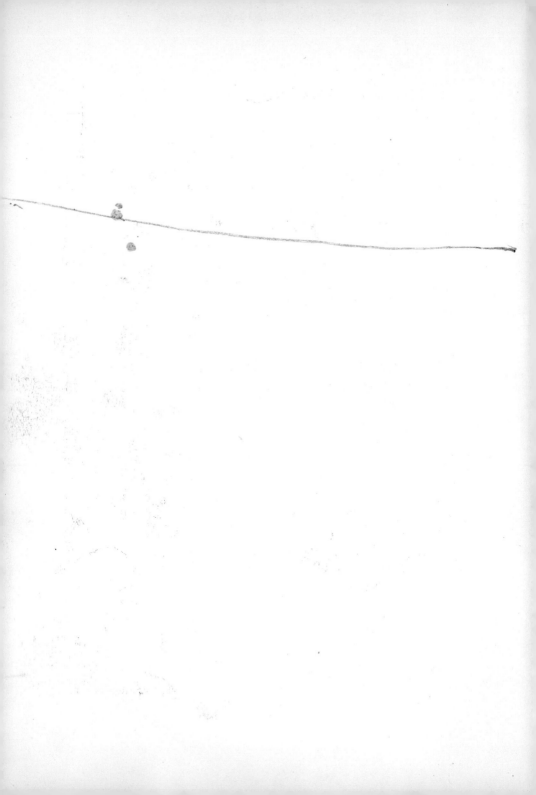

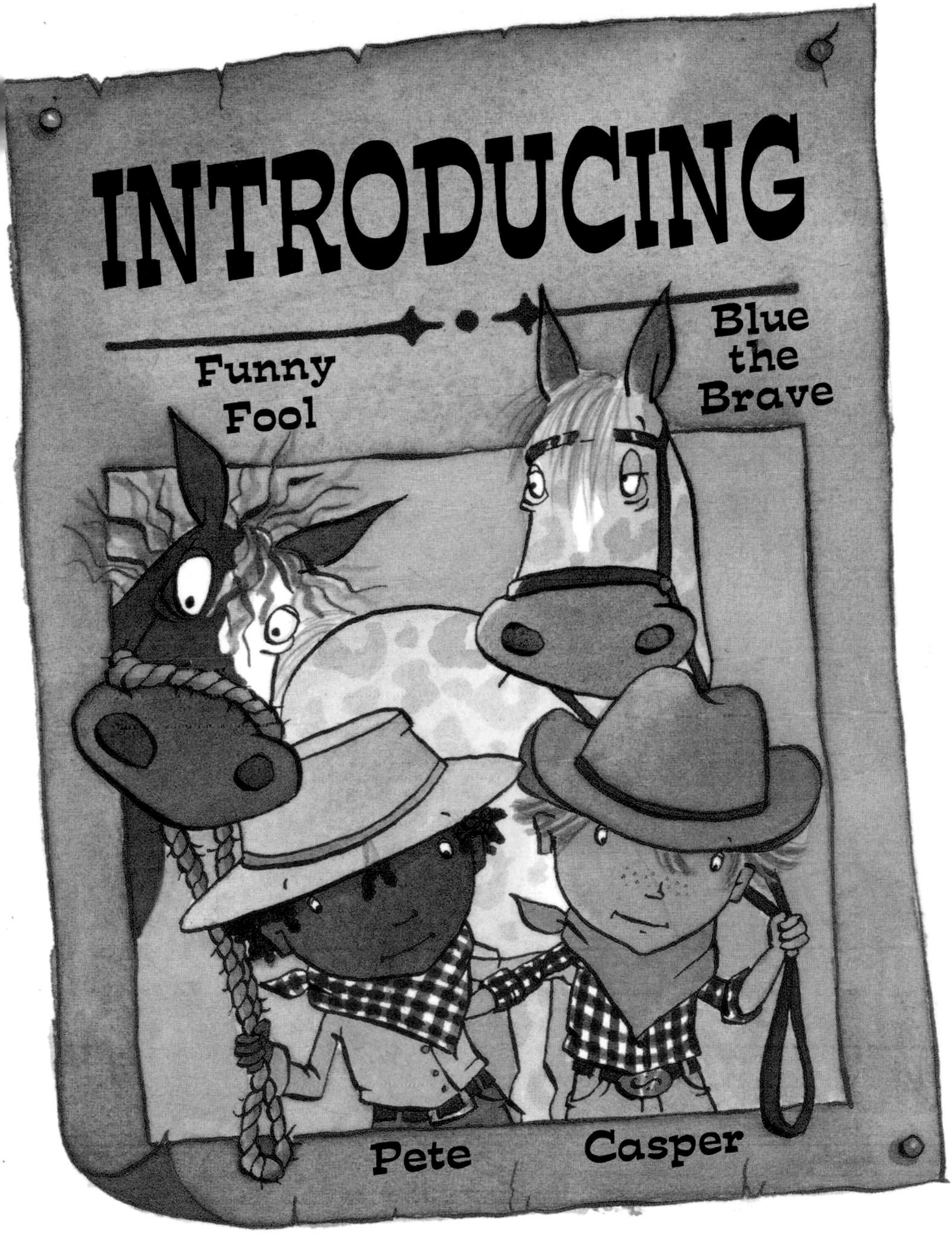
INTRODUCING
Funny Fool
Blue the Brave
Pete
Casper

For Katie
C.C.

To Freddie – hope you have lots
of fun adventures, yeehah! x
J.McC.

Reading Consultant: Prue Goodwin, Lecturer in literacy and children's books

ORCHARD BOOKS
338 Euston Road, London NW1 3BH
Orchard Books Australia
Hachette Children's Books
Level 17/207 Kent Street, Sydney NSW 2000

First published in 2011 by Orchard Books
First paperback publication in 2012

Text © Catherine Coe 2011
Illustrations © Jan McCafferty 2011

ISBN 978 1 40830 689 5 (hardback)
ISBN 978 1 40830 697 0 (paperback)

1 3 5 7 9 10 8 6 4 2 (hardback)
1 3 5 7 9 10 8 6 4 2 (paperback)

Printed in China

Orchard Books is a division of Hachette Children's Books,
an Hachette UK company.

www.hachette.co.uk

KID COWBOY

Wild West Walk

Written by
Catherine Coe

Illustrated by
Jan McCafferty

ORCHARD

Casper the Kid Cowboy had woken up extra early today. He was *very* excited. Casper and his best friend, Pete, were going on an adventure to the Wild West!

Casper and Pete couldn't decide what they needed. So they took almost *everything*:

their tent . . .

buckets and spades . . .

a kite . . .

and even their suitcases!

It was lucky that their horses, Funny Fool and Blue the Brave, were very strong!

"Let's go!" cried Casper.

The two cowboys set off, as fast as they could go.

But it wasn't very fast . . .

After a while, they reached a crossroads.

"Oh no!" Casper said. "We packed everything – except the map!"

"I'm sure we'll find the Wild West without a map," Pete said. "Let's go this way."
He pointed left.

But by lunchtime, the cowboys
still hadn't found the Wild West.
"I'm hungry," Pete complained.
"Let's make a campfire and cook
some food."

"Great idea, partner!" Casper
replied.

They gathered some firewood,
and heated up some
baked beans.

After their lunch, the two cowboys were no longer hungry. But Pete was *very* noisy. And smelly!

Casper couldn't stand too close
to him.
"I think I had too many
beans!" Pete said.

"Let's get out of here,"
Casper said.

But Pete's horse, Funny Fool,
didn't want to be near smelly
Pete either!

Finally they mounted their horses. They rode for hours. It was getting dark, but the Wild West was still nowhere in sight!

"We'll have to set up camp soon," Pete decided.

"OK, partner!" Casper was excited. He'd never slept in a tent before!

It took a *long* time to put up
the tent. Pete didn't think he
needed the instructions, but
Casper thought they might
have been useful!

Blue the Brave and Funny Fool
were a bit too big for the tent,
but they didn't seem to mind.
It wasn't long before everyone
was asleep.

The next morning, Casper and Pete were determined to find the Wild West. They set off as soon as the sun rose.

They quickly reached a river –
but there was no way around it!
"We'll have to gallop through,"
Pete said to his best friend.

Casper wasn't so sure. But he really wanted to get to the Wild West, so he rode to the water's edge.

"You can do it," Pete shouted
from the other side.

"Come on, boy," Casper said
to his horse.

Casper and Blue soon found
out how much fun it was to
splash through the water!

The two cowboys and their horses kept going.

"What's that?" Casper said suddenly. Ahead was the biggest rock he had ever seen. Casper gazed up . . . and up . . . and up. It looked a bit scary.

"It's a canyon," Pete said.

"Let's find a way through!"

Casper soon forgot his fear. Weaving through the canyon felt like a great adventure!

"Yee-ha!" cried the cowboys, as they emerged from the canyon. But there was still no sign of the Wild West.

"Where is it?" cried Casper.
He wished they'd remembered
the map.

But Pete wouldn't give up.
"What's that?" he said. He could
see something in the distance.
It was a *huge* map.
"At last!" Casper said.
They looked closely.

"We were in the Wild West the whole time!" Pete exclaimed.

"No wonder it was so much fun!" Casper replied.

"So we've had our Wild West adventure, after all!" Pete said, patting his horse.
"We sure have, partner!"
Casper grinned.

As the sun set on another day, the cowboys headed for home, knowing that the next time they wanted to go to the Wild West, it wasn't far away.
It was all around them!

Written by **Illustrated by**
Catherine Coe   **Jan McCafferty**

All priced at £8.99

Orchard Books are available from all good bookshops,
or can be ordered from our website: www.orchardbooks.co.uk,
or telephone 01235 827702, or fax 01235 827703.

Prices and availability are subject to change.